D0478800

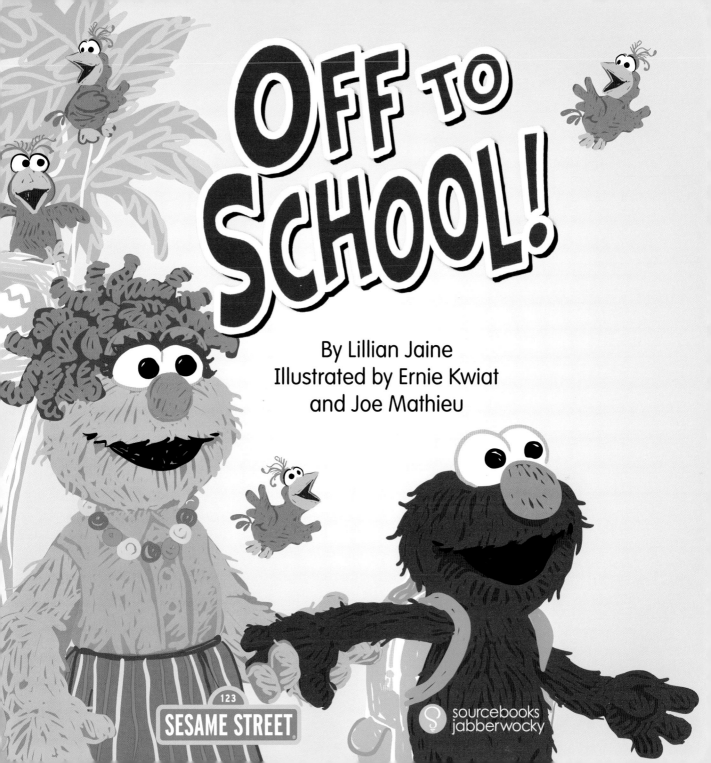

OFF TO SCHOOL!

By Lillian Jaine
Illustrated by Ernie Kwiat
and Joe Mathieu

123
SESAME STREET®

sourcebooks
jabberwocky

Tomorrow is Elmo's first day of school!

Elmo wants to go to sleep, but there are funny butterflies in Elmo's tummy!

Elmo would feel better if you rubbed his tummy.

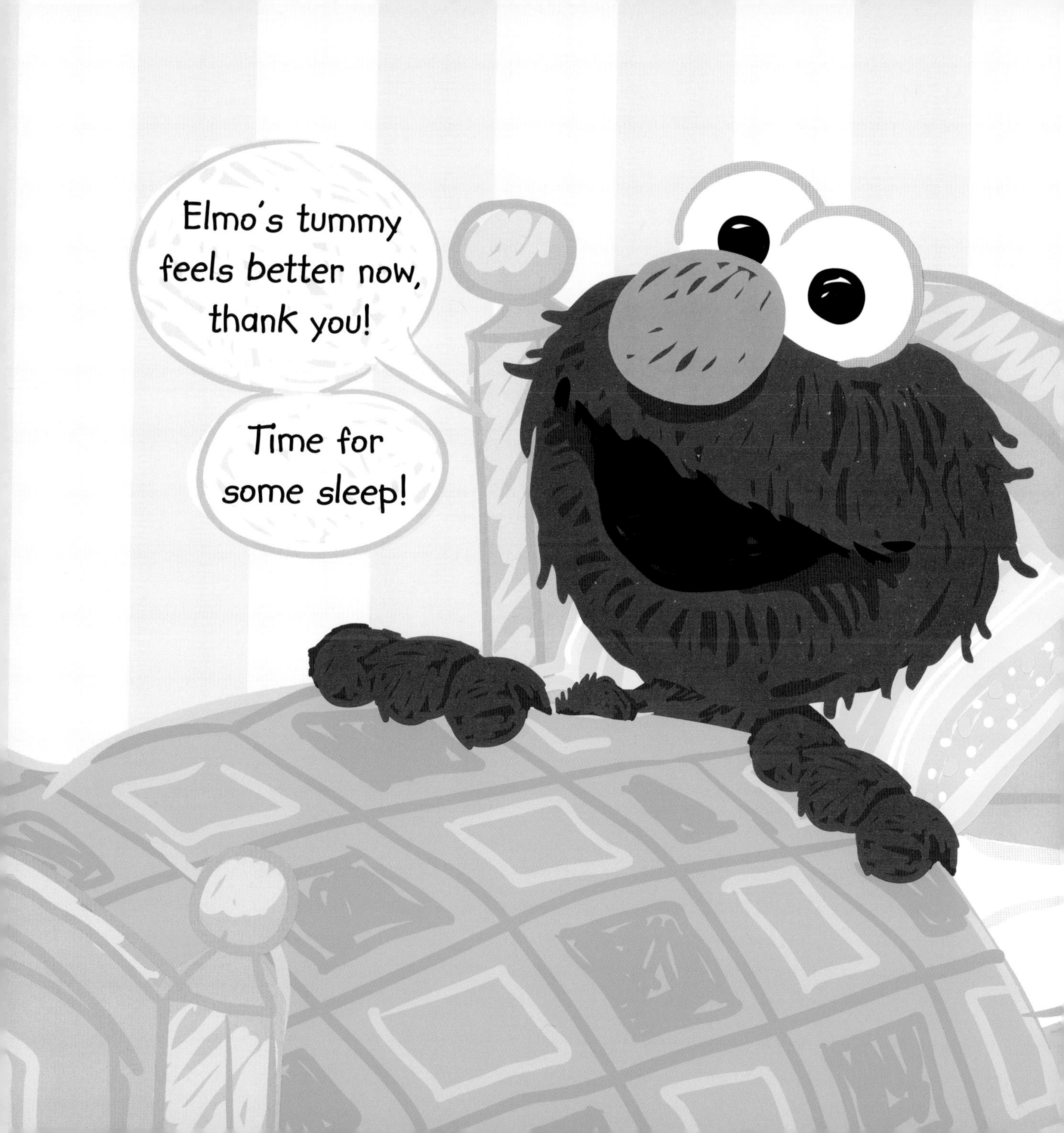
Elmo's tummy feels better now, thank you!
Time for some sleep!

What a beautiful morning!
Reach your hands up high
and stretch with Elmo!

First, Elmo has to eat breakfast. Elmo wants his mind and body to be strong for his big day!

Help Elmo pour his cereal by tapping the box.

Thank you!

Elmo is feeling full of energy. Now it's time to get Elmo's backpack and lunch ready!

Uh-oh, Elmo's belly butterflies are back. Elmo is still nervous about the first day of school.

Can you rub Elmo's tummy again?

Hee hee hee!
That tickles!

Elmo and Mommy are
filling Elmo's backpack
with school supplies and
some special items.

Elmo has Baby David's little tiny blanket.
Mommy says if Elmo is lonely at school,
Elmo can hold the blanket and feel all
warm and cozy!

Touch the blanket
with Elmo!

Elmo wants to make sure
Baby David is okay while
Elmo is at school.

Elmo will give Baby David
a big hug.

Say, "Have a good
day, Baby David!"

Look, a picture of Mommy and Elmo!

If Elmo misses Mommy, Elmo can look at the picture and feel better!

Help Elmo put the picture inside Elmo's lunch box!

Press hard so it doesn't fall out!

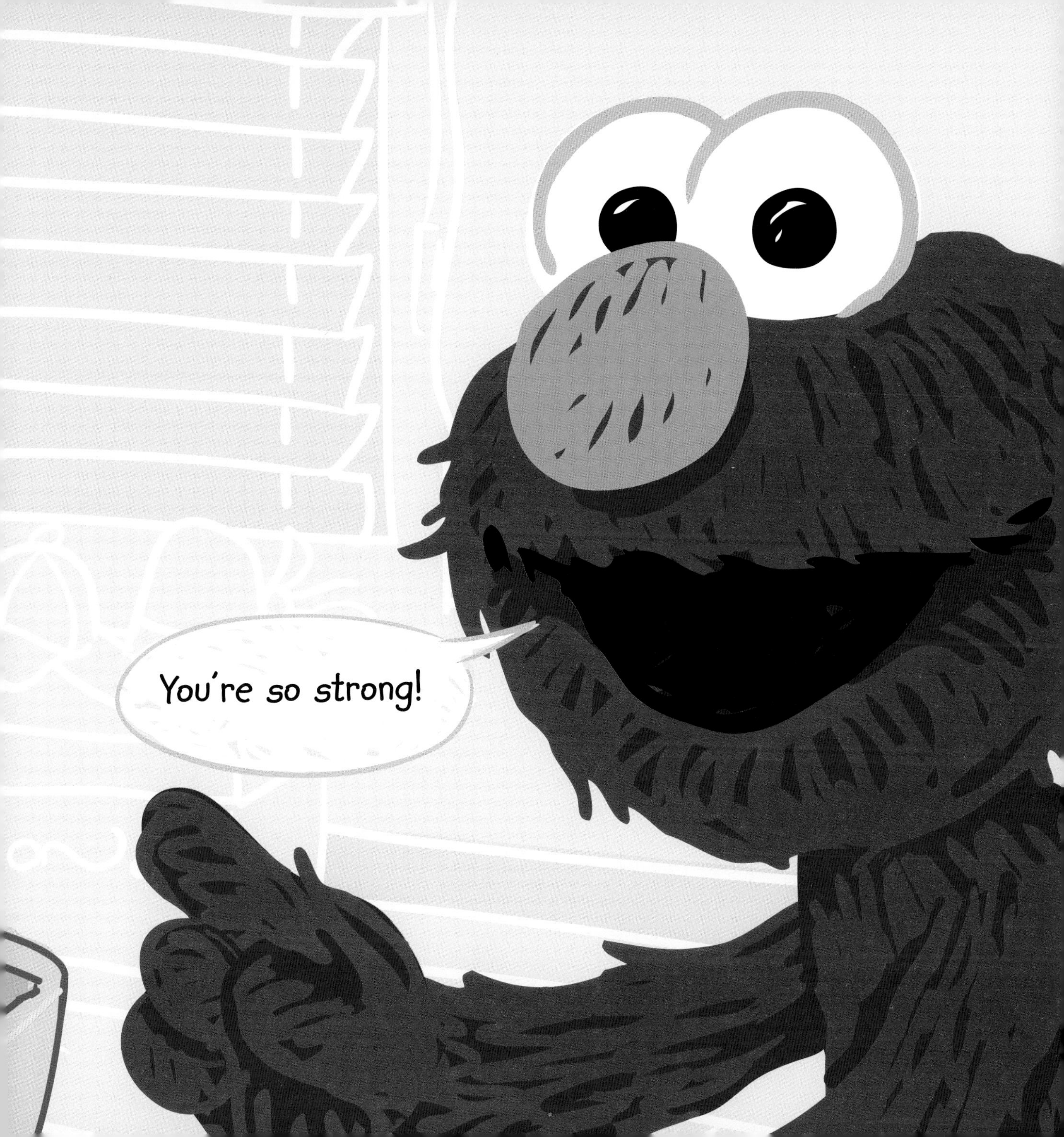
You're so strong!

Now it's time to go, but Elmo is getting nervous again.

Elmo's heart feels like it's going boom-boom-a-boom.

Elmo needs to belly breathe.

Put your hands on
Elmo's tummy.

Breathe in deep,
then breathe out
nice and slow.

You are a very good belly breather!
Now Elmo will say good-bye to Daddy,
and Mommy and Elmo will walk to the
bus stop together.

Elmo thinks it is a beautiful day.

Look, all the little birds are getting ready to go to school, too!

Here comes the school bus!
Everyone is ready to go.

Have fun!
Mommy loves you!

Help Elmo say good-bye to Mommy with hugs and kisses!

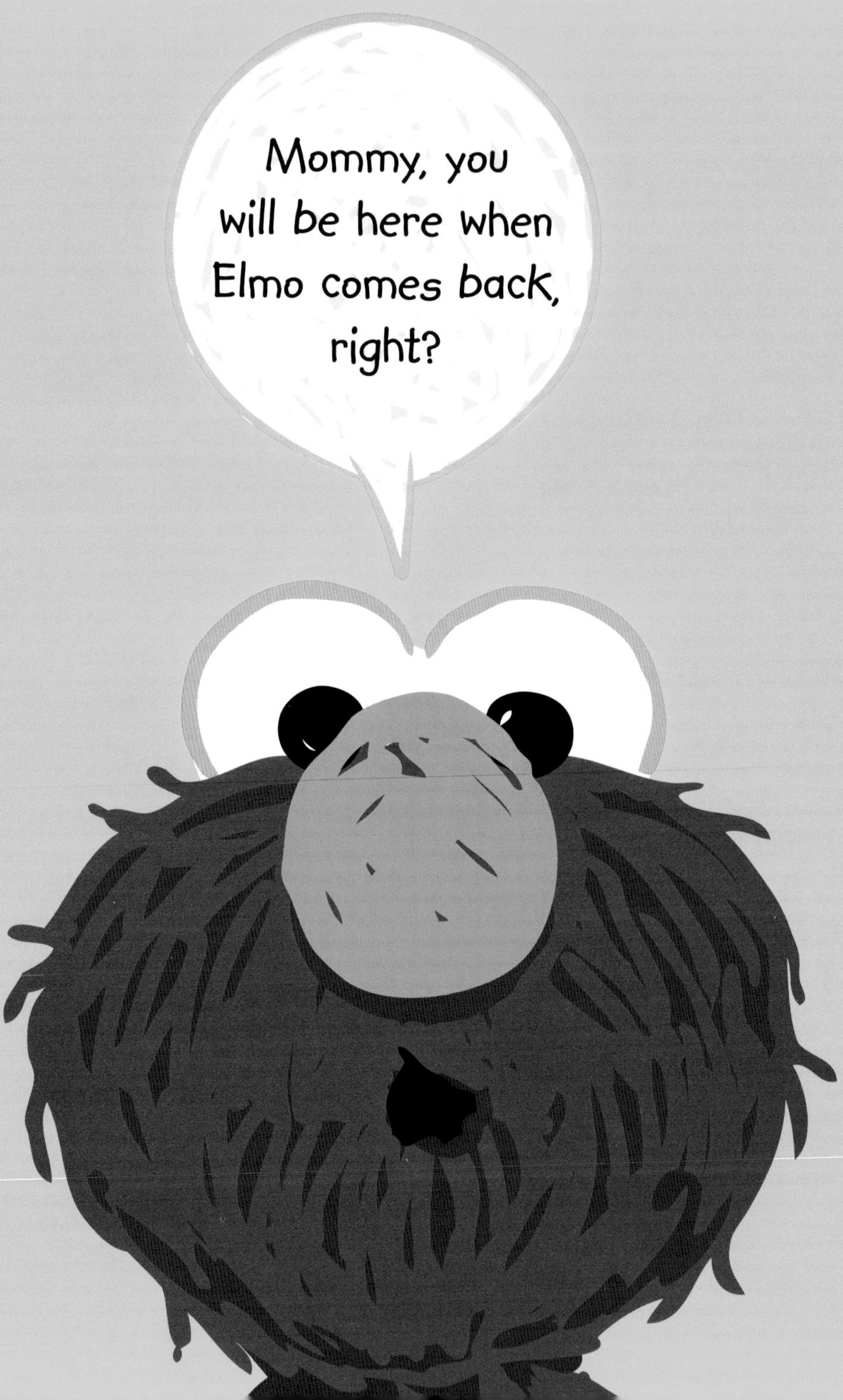
Mommy, you will be here when Elmo comes back, right?

Elmo is nervous but also excited to go to school!

Elmo told you it was going to be an exciting day!

Cover and internal design © 2015 by Sourcebooks, Inc.

Cover illustrations © Sesame Workshop
Text by Lillian Jaine
Internal illustrations by Ernie Kwiat
Cover illustration by Joe Mathieu

Published by Sourcebooks Jabberwocky, an imprint of Sourcebooks, Inc.
P.O. Box 4410, Naperville, Illinois 60567-4410
(630) 961-3900
Fax: (630) 961-2168
www.jabberwockykids.com

Library of Congress Cataloging-in-Publication data is on file with the publisher

Source of Production: Worzalla, Stevens Point WI, USA
Date of Production: May 2015
Run Number: 5003860

Printed and bound in the United States of America.
WOZ 10 9 8 7 6 5 4 3 2 1